To Louis Pascal

First edition for the United States published by
Barron's Educational Series, Inc., 2000

First published in Great Britain in 2000 by
The Bodley Head Children's Books, Random House,
20 Vauxhall Bridge Road, London, SW1V 2SA

Text and illustrations copyright © John Prater 2000

All inquiries should be addressed to:
Barron's Educational Series, Inc.
250 Wireless Boulevard
Hauppauge, New York 11788
http://www.barronseduc.com

Library of Congress Catalog Card No.: 99-68444
International Standard Book No.: 0-7641-5279-3

Printed in Hong Kong
9 8 7 6 5 4 3

AGAIN!

JOHN PRATER

BARRON'S

It was a lovely sunny day and Grandbear was enjoying the warm sunshine when a little voice said, "Play with me, play with me." It was Baby Bear, and Baby Bear wanted to play.

So Grandbear climbed
out of the hammock,

and together they
built a tower out of
Baby Bear's blocks.

Baby Bear pushed them over.

CLATTER!
CRASH!

"AGAIN!"
said Baby Bear.

So they built
an even bigger
tower of blocks,

and Baby Bear
pushed them
over once more.
**CLATTER!
CRASH!**

"**AGAIN!**" said Baby Bear.
"Are you sure?" asked Grandbear,
who was getting a bit tired of
this game.
"**AGAIN!**" said Baby Bear.

So together they built
the biggest tower they
could using all the blocks.

Baby Bear pushed them all over for a third time.
CLATTER! CRASH!

"AGAIN!" said Baby Bear.
"No," said Grandbear, "let's do
something else."

They went over to the sandbox,
and with a little help from Grandbear,
Baby Bear made a sandcastle.

Baby Bear had great
fun stamping it down.
STAMP! STOMP!

"AGAIN!"
said Baby Bear.

So they filled the bucket
lots of times, and made
a big sandcastle.

This took a lot of stamping down.

STAMP! STOMP!

"AGAIN!"said Baby Bear.
"Are you sure?" asked
Grandbear who was
getting very tired of
this game by now.
"AGAIN!" said
Baby Bear.

So they filled the bucket lots and lots of times until they had
made the biggest sandcastle ever.

And what did Baby Bear do?

"**AGAIN!**"said Baby Bear.
"No, no," said Grandbear.

"Let's do something useful. Let's water the plants."

So Grandbear filled
the watering cans,
and they watered
the smallest plants.
PLIP! DRIP!

The watering cans
were soon empty.

"AGAIN!"
said Baby Bear.

Grandbear filled the watering can again, and Baby Bear watered the bigger plants. DRIP! DROP!
"AGAIN!" said Baby Bear.

Then, using the hose, Baby Bear watered
the biggest plants. **DRIP! DROP!**
"AGAIN!" said Baby Bear when Grandbear
turned off the tap.

"No, no, no," puffed Grandbear.
"You've watered everything.
Let's do something else."
Grandbear made a cold
drink, and found Baby
Bear's biggest
and best storybook.

Then together,
they clambered
into the hammock.

Grandbear read the story all the way through from beginning to end.
"AGAIN!" said Baby Bear.

But Grandbear's eyes were beginning to close.
Baby Bear gave Grandbear a kiss and a cuddle.
"Again," murmured Grandbear, sleepily.
And so Baby Bear hugged Grandbear again...

and again...

and again.